The Ballad of Belle Dorcas

by *William H. Hooks*
illustrated by *Brian Pinkney*

ALFRED A. KNOPF NEW YORK

Text copyright © 1990 by William H. Hooks.
Illustrations copyright © 1990 by Brian Pinkney.
All rights reserved under International and Pan-American
Copyright Conventions. Published in the United States by
Alfred A. Knopf, Inc., New York, and simultaneously in Canada
by Random House of Canada Limited, Toronto. Distributed by
Random House, Inc., New York.

Book design by Mina Greenstein
2   4   6   8   10   9   7   5   3   1
Manufactured in Singapore

Library of Congress Cataloging-in-Publication Data
Hooks, William H. The ballad of Belle Dorcas / by William H.
Hooks ; illustrated by Brian Pinkney.   p.   cm.
Summary: When she falls in love with Joshua, a slave, freeborn Belle
Dorcas uses the magic of a conjure woman to keep Joshua with her.
ISBN 0-394-84645-1   ISBN 0-394-94645-6
[1. Afro-Americans—Fiction.   2. Slavery—Fiction.   3. Magic—
Fiction]   I. Pinkney, Brian, ill.   II. Title.   PZ7.H7664Bal
1990 [Fic]—dc19   89-2715

For my friends,
Dorothy Carter and Lucia Jack
—W.H.H.

To Andrea
—B.P.

AUTHOR'S NOTE

The Ballad of Belle Dorcas is based on one of the many conjure tales that I listened to with awe and tantalizing shivers during my childhood. Such tales abound in the tidewater sections of the Carolinas. And a rare conjure (pronounced "cunger" locally) man or woman can still be found today, primarily among the Gullah people who live along the Carolina coast and in the offshore rice islands. Conjurers were both feared and respected—feared for the powerful spells they could cast and respected for the protection they could afford one from spells. Their spells ran the gamut from good to evil, and the same conjurer might cast spells of both sorts. To reinforce spells conjurers used such elements as roots, herbs, dried blood, hair, powdered insects, reptiles, and bones, not to mention a generous dollop of the power of suggestion. In fact, essential to the conjurer's spell casting was the complete belief on the part of all involved that the spell would work. As the belief in the power of conjurers diminished over the years, so did their power and number. What remains is a fascinating body of conjure tales that continue to flourish in the oral tradition of the Carolinas.

The term "free issue" refers to the offspring between slave masters and slave women, children who were given their freedom at birth. Free-issue people found themselves in a nether world, for they were neither slaves nor full-fledged citizens. They tended to be clannish and often intermarried with other free issues. In eastern North Carolina, early in the nineteenth century, they formed a community called East Arcadia. Many of their descendants still live on the farms established there by their forebears more than one hundred fifty years ago.

THE BALLAD OF BELLE DORCAS

1

BELLE DORCAS was pretty as her name, and no slave either. Belle Dorcas was free issue, her daddy being a white master, her mama being his house slave. Belle Dorcas had papers given by her natural daddy at birth, making her free.

Her mama set great store on having a free-issue child, a daughter born free. From the time she could remember, Belle Dorcas's mama told her about the things she could do. "Belle, Belle, my pretty Belle," she said, "you're free issue, child, and you can come and go free as a hummingbird. No slave master has rights over you. You be free to even learn letters and numbers and read books." It was her mama's dream that Belle would grow up and marry a fine young man from the free-issue settlement on the Wilmington road. "No slave cabin for you, sugar," said her mama. "You'll live in your own house on your own piece of land."

And in the right season many free-issue men came down the dusty Wilmington road. All summer long they courted Belle Dorcas, bringing flowers, horehound candy, and blood-red pomegranates. They plied her with fancy words. But Belle Dorcas favored none of them.

Belle Dorcas loved Joshua. Always had, for as long as she could remember. But Joshua was a slave. And a highly prized slave at that. Joshua was the hardest-working man on the plantation and the best fiddle player in the county. The master sent him to neighboring plantations to play for parties, holidays, and weddings. He always came back with a few coins in his pocket. He dreamed that someday he would have enough saved to buy his freedom and marry Belle.

When the rains of fall had settled the dust on the Wilmington road and Belle Dorcas had chosen no free-issue man, she spoke with her mama.

"Dear Mama, I'm breaking your heart, and you are crushing mine. I'd rather live with Joshua as a slave than as free issue with another man. It's him I'll marry or die." From that day on Belle Dorcas took no food and spoke to no one. She sat flat on the porch with her knees drawn up and her arms hugging them tight, staring straight ahead. For a week she sat.

Finally her mama went to the master. "Sir," she said, "I fear Belle Dorcas will die, lest she marry Joshua."

"I'm overly fond of the girl," he said. "And I know your heart was set on a free-issue man for her. But let her marry Joshua and live in the slave quarters."

It was done. Joshua took all of the coins he had saved from his fiddle playing and bought Belle Dorcas a pair of fine gold earrings. Belle Dorcas and Joshua were happy—happy as slaves could be. But when three full moons had waxed and waned and it was summer again, the master was thrown from his horse. He died the day after.

The new master cared only for money. He sold great pieces of the land. Then his eye fell on the slaves. There were far more than he needed now. He picked the strongest young men, Joshua among them, to be offered up for sale on the auction block.

Belle Dorcas pleaded with the master. "Spare Joshua, sir, I pray you." But her pleas did not move him. "Then sell me with Joshua, that we may go together," she begged. The master laughed and said, "You're free issue, Belle. I can't sell you."

The slaves were to be sold in two days. Belle Dorcas was frantic. She could think of no way to save Joshua. Unless . . . Unless she could get help from Granny Lizard. Granny Lizard was a cunger woman, a free-issue cunger woman who lived on the Wilmington road.

Granny Lizard was famed for her spells and root working. But her price was high. And Belle Dorcas had no money. What could she offer for a spell so powerful that it could save Joshua? Her gold earrings—the only gift she had from him.

2

BELLE DORCAS ran through the noonday heat five miles down the Wilmington road. She pounded on Granny Lizard's door. She was afraid of the old woman but more afraid for Joshua. "Door's open," croaked a high-pitched voice. "I was expecting you."

Belle Dorcas stepped into the dark cabin. "You're my only hope!" she cried. "You've got to save Joshua! Keep him here. Don't let them sell him south!" She poured out the whole story. Granny Lizard listened with her small, round eyes half-closed and her pointy tongue flickering across her lips.

"You're asking for a powerful spell," said the old woman. "It can be done if gold presses my hand."

"Here is gold," said Belle Dorcas, thrusting the earrings into Granny Lizard's hand.

"There's still a question I must put to you," said the cunger woman. "Can you give up Joshua to keep him?"

Belle Dorcas said, "Yes," without even thinking on the strange question.

Then Granny Lizard made her spell, a cunger bag no bigger than a locket. "Walk with Joshua in the woods tonight," she said. "When you are hidden by the trees, rub the cunger bag around his neck, and he will never leave the plantation."

Belle Dorcas told Joshua none of this, for Granny Lizard had warned her that the spell must be kept secret from all. So Joshua went walking with Belle on what he thought to be their last night together. And when they were deep in the woods he took her in his arms and kissed her.

It was then Belle Dorcas cast the spell. She quickly rubbed the cunger bag around Joshua's neck. He trembled and laughed. "You're tickling me," he said. Then he began to shake all over. His feet dug into the ground and his arms began to rise.

"Joshua!" cried Belle Dorcas. "What is happening to you?" Joshua made no answer. He only shook and trembled. As Belle Dorcas watched, his feet rooted into the ground, his arms sprouted leaves, and bark covered his body.

Belle Dorcas drew back in horror. Joshua was becoming a tree, a great cedar tree, with red bark and dark green foliage. She threw her arms around the tree and called, "Joshua! Joshua!" But there was no answer. The Joshua tree stood silent and still.

Through the starless night Belle Dorcas ran the five miles back to Granny Lizard. "What have you done?" she screamed. "What have you done to my Joshua?"

"You wanted he should never leave," said the cunger woman. "You got your wish. I said you would have to give him up."

"I don't understand," Belle cried. "I gave you gold. You only gave me grief."

Granny Lizard grabbed Belle Dorcas and shook her hard. "Now, listen to me careful, girl. I said you would have to give him up in order to keep him." The cunger woman spoke softly. "This is how you get your Joshua back. Go at night to the cedar tree. Rub the cunger bag around it and the tree will change back to Joshua. At daybreak you must bring him back and let him be a tree again."

The next day the master put out the alarm. Joshua was
missing. "Bring the bloodhounds! Make a search!" he cried.
"No slave has ever escaped from this plantation." But no
trace of Joshua was found. When the master saw Belle
Dorcas's tears, he never dreamed they were tears of joy.

Granny Lizard's spell had worked, just as she said it would.
Every night Belle went to the woods, where she changed the
Joshua tree into the Joshua man. And they were happy again,
with the half-a-life Granny Lizard's spell had given them.

3

Season followed season, and no one guessed there was a Joshua tree. Then the master gave an order to the slaves. "The smokehouse needs a new roof. This time cover it with cedar shakes, shingles that will last forever. Go to the woods. Cut the largest cedar tree you can find."

Belle Dorcas was in the woods that day, picking huckleberries for Joshua's midnight dinner. At first she heard a moaning sound like a ringing in her ears. Then she heard the whack of chopping and the bite of axes cutting into wood. She ran to the Joshua tree just as the great cedar came crashing down.

"Joshua!" she screamed, and threw herself onto the fallen cedar. The slaves drew back in puzzlement at the wailing woman hugging the tree. Finally they pulled her away and dragged the tree out of the woods. Belle Dorcas followed, screaming, "You've killed my Joshua!"

They split the tree into cedar shakes and covered the
smokehouse roof. Everyone thought Belle Dorcas was crazy,
with her mad ravings about Joshua and the cedar tree. She
wandered the woods by day. At night she circled the
smokehouse talking to herself. Soon the children were calling
her Crazy Belle.

4

At Christmastime Cook sent Pompey, the master's houseboy, to the smokehouse to cut down a sugar-cured ham. But Pompey came running back, declaring he heard moaning there. Cook scolded him, then went to see for herself.

There was no doubt about it. Cook heard it too. A dreadful moaning and groaning was coming from the smokehouse. They told the master. He didn't believe it. "A smokehouse that moans! What nonsense!" he exclaimed.

But all through the winter no slave went to the smokehouse alone. They entered by twos, got what they needed, and hurried away from the pitiful cries. Only the children and Crazy Belle seemed not to mind the noises.

Then one gusty, rainy night, when the master was riding home, he saw the smokehouse door open, banging in the wind. He rode over. But his horse shied and backed away, for as the door moved it made a sound like groaning. A shiver of fear snaked up the master's back.

Now he was convinced that his slaves were not lying. Still, he didn't want them thinking that their master was afraid. The next day he gave an order. "Move that cursed smokehouse! Move it deep into the woods. What good is a smokehouse that a bunch of superstitious slaves are afraid to enter?"

So it happened that the smokehouse came back to the place where the Joshua tree was cut. Belle Dorcas moved there as soon as she heard. And there she stayed, talking to the smokehouse all day long. At night she thought she heard fiddle music from far off. She wandered the plantation, following the sound, calling, "Joshua, Joshua, where are you?" again and again.

One night Belle Dorcas followed the fiddle music far down the Wilmington road, until she came to Granny Lizard's cabin. She had no gold to offer, but she knocked anyway. "Come in," croaked a high voice. "I've been expecting you."

Belle Dorcas was truly near mad by now. It took Granny Lizard some time to calm her down and make her listen carefully. "You've forgotten what I said about the spell. You had to give him up in order to keep him."

Belle Dorcas shook her head. "I've lost him for good!" she cried. The old woman cackled. "The cunger bag still works," she said. "You can still get your Joshua back. You've given him up long enough. Let me whisper in your ear what you must do."

Belle Dorcas ran the full five miles back to the smokehouse. She rubbed the cunger bag around the outside of the house. Then she stepped through the door. There stood Joshua with his fiddle in his hand, smiling and holding out his arms.

And from that time on Belle Dorcas and Joshua were together every night until they were very old. When Belle Dorcas died, the smokehouse disappeared. Where it stood, two young cedar trees were found growing side by side.

WILLIAM H. HOOKS was born and raised in the tidewater area of rural North Carolina, where *The Ballad of Belle Dorcas* takes place. Now the Director of Publications at Bank Street College of Education, he often makes visits to North Carolina, where he collects folklore. He is the successful author of more than 25 children's books, and lives in New York City.

BRIAN PINKNEY's education began at home, where he was surrounded by the illustrations of his father, Jerry Pinkney. He went on to receive an M.F.A. from the School of Visual Arts. While working on his degree, he illustrated two children's books that have recently been published; *The Ballad of Belle Dorcas* is his third. Of it he says, "I was interested in illustrating this book to research and understand my past as an African-American in this country." Brian Pinkney lives in New York City.